PRESENTS

THE AMERICAN GIRLS
COLLECTION

KIRSTEN
1854

MEET KIRSTEN · An American Girl

KIRSTEN LEARNS A LESSON · A School Story

KIRSTEN'S SURPRISE · A Christmas Story

SAMANTHA
1904

MEET SAMANTHA · An American Girl

SAMANTHA LEARNS A LESSON · A School Story

SAMANTHA'S SURPRISE · A Christmas Story

MOLLY
1944

MEET MOLLY · An American Girl

MOLLY LEARNS A LESSON · A School Story

MOLLY'S SURPRISE · A Christmas Story

KIRSTEN
LEARNS
A LESSON
A SCHOOL STORY

BY JANET SHAW

ILLUSTRATIONS RENÉE GRAEF

VIGNETTES PAUL LACKNER

PLEASANT COMPANY

PICTURE CREDITS
The following individuals and organizations have generously given
permission to reprint illustrations contained in "Looking Back:"
pp. 64–65—State Historical Society of Wisconsin; Minnesota Historical
Society; State Historical Society of Wisconsin; State Historical Society of
Wisconsin; p. 67—*Harper's*, September 19, 1884, Minnesota Historical
Society Collection; pp. 68–69—E. L. Henry, *Country School*, Yale University
Art Gallery, The Mabel Brady Garvan Collection; Potlatch Corporation,
Northwest Paper, Courtesy Minnesota Historical Society; State Historical
Society of Wisconsin; Minnesota Historical Society.

Edited by Jeanne Thieme
Designed by Myland McRevey

Library of Congress Cataloging-in-Publication Data

Shaw, Janet Beeler, 1937–
Kirsten learns a lesson: a school story

(The American girls collection)
Summary: After immigrating from Sweden to join relatives in an
American prairie community, Kirsten endures the ordeal of a strange
school through a secret friendship with an Indian girl.
[1. Swedish Americans—Fiction. 2. Emigration and immigration—
Fiction. 3. Frontier and pioneer life—Fiction. 4. Indians of
North America—Fiction. 5. Schools—Fiction]
I. Graef, Renée, ill. II. Title. III. Series.
PZ7.S53423Ki 1986   [Fic]   86-60622
ISBN 0-937295-09-4
ISBN 0-937295-10-8 (pbk.)

FOR MY MOTHER,
NADINA FOWLER

TABLE OF CONTENTS

KIRSTEN'S FAMILY
AND FRIENDS

CHAPTER ONE
MISS WINSTON 1

CHAPTER TWO
A SECRET FRIEND 19

CHAPTER THREE
VISITORS 30

CHAPTER FOUR
SINGING BIRD AND YELLOW HAIR 38

CHAPTER FIVE
BELONGING 46

LOOKING BACK 63

KIRSTEN'S FAMILY

KIRSTEN

A nine-year-old who moves with her family to a new home on America's frontier in 1854.

SINGING BIRD

Kirsten's secret Indian friend, who calls her "Yellow Hair."

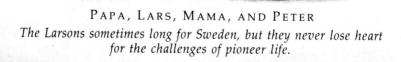

PAPA, LARS, MAMA, AND PETER

The Larsons sometimes long for Sweden, but they never lose heart for the challenges of pioneer life.

...AND FRIENDS

MISS WINSTON
Kirsten's teacher, who helps her learn English.

MARTA
Kirsten's best friend on the long trip from Sweden to Minnesota.

ANNA, AUNT INGER, LISBETH, AND UNCLE OLAV
Kirsten's American relatives live on a new farm in Minnesota, where they make the Larson family feel at home.

MISS WINSTON

TINE

Kirsten hurried down the path beside her cousin Lisbeth. In one hand she carried a lunch in her wooden tine. With the other she held her shawl tightly around her shoulders.

"You're walking too fast!" Kirsten said.

But Lisbeth didn't slow down. "Mr. Coogan will be angry if we're late. He's really strict," she answered. Lisbeth was eleven. Mr. Coogan had been her teacher since she was nine. She loved to tell stories about how fierce he was. In fact ever since July, when Kirsten and her family had come to live on Uncle Olav's farm, Lisbeth and her sister Anna had talked about Mr. Coogan and Powderkeg

1

School. Now it was November. The harvest was over and it was time for the fall term to begin. Today would be Kirsten's first day in an American school.

Kirsten walked as fast as she could to keep up with Lisbeth's longer stride. Her boots puffed up dust.

Anna, who was just seven, tagged farther behind. "Wait for me," she called. "I want to stop for a drink of water."

Kirsten and Lisbeth stopped beside the stream. A light mist rose from the clear water, and a few yellow leaves floated on it. Kirsten stopped and put her fingertip into a deer track in the sand. How she wished she could stay here by the stream instead of going to school.

"If you mind him, Mr. Coogan will like you," Lisbeth said. "But he gets really angry when the big boys fight."

"In Sweden the boys weren't allowed to fight in school," Kirsten said.

Lisbeth smiled and tossed her head. "Well, this is America, and here the boys get wild whether

they should or not. Sometimes Mr. Coogan hits them with a cane. Once he punched Amos Anderson with his fist! If you talk back to Mr. Coogan, he swats your hand with his ruler."

Anna wiped her mouth on the back of her hand. Her round cheeks were rosy from running along the path. "He's mean! But he'll never hit you, Kirsten. You're too nice. Don't worry."

Kirsten let out a long breath. "I'm not really worried," she said softly. But she was dizzy, the way she'd felt on the ship just before she was seasick.

"Does your stomach hurt?" Anna asked. "When I'm scared, my stomach hurts and flutters like there's a bird inside me."

Kirsten put her hand to her waist. Yes, her stomach did feel full of wings. Butterflies, maybe. And she hadn't been able to eat the pancakes Mama made for breakfast. "My stomach hurts a little," she admitted.

"I was really scared the first day I went to school," Anna said. "I wondered if the others would like me. It's hard to be the new girl."

Lisbeth slipped her arm through Kirsten's as

they started along the path again. "Just do what we do, Kirsten. You'll get along fine in school."

Kirsten sighed. "But I can't do what you do. I only speak a little bit of English, and I can't read a word of it. I won't fit in at all." How she wished she were back in her village in Sweden, where she knew everyone and everyone knew her and they all spoke the same language.

"School only lasts until four o'clock," Anna added. "When it's over, we can stop at our fort and play for a few minutes." She darted off to hide their dolls in the secret hideaway under the cherry tree. On her way back, she broke off a sprig of bittersweet and handed Kirsten a few of the waxy red berries.

"We can put these berries on our doll cakes," Kirsten said.

"Come on!" Lisbeth said. "I hear the school bell." She began to run.

And suddenly, before Kirsten was ready, they were in the clearing in front of the large log cabin that was Powderkeg School. The last children were just going in the door.

Powderkeg School didn't look very different

 from the log cabin Kirsten and her family lived in on Uncle Olav's farm. But the school had more windows, and a stove pipe stuck up in the center of the roof.

"There's the outhouse," Anna said. She pointed to a small shed behind the log cabin. "Girls use it before boys do at recess. I won't let any boys peek at you, I promise."

Kirsten hadn't thought of *that!* What a lot of things she had to worry about! She peered around Lisbeth's shoulder into the schoolhouse. Children were finding places to sit on the benches that lined the walls. Only her brothers, Lars and Peter, looked familiar. Lars sat with the other big boys. Peter was with the younger boys, some even smaller than he.

Kirsten took a deep breath, as though she were about to dive into the stream. She followed Anna and Lisbeth through the door.

Lisbeth pulled off her shawl and hung it on a peg. Kirsten draped hers over it. For a moment she let her forehead rest against the comforting wool that smelled of woodsmoke. Then she turned and looked around.

A pot-bellied wood stove sat in the open space in the center of the room. But instead of the fearsome Mr. Coogan, a young woman in a black dress sat on the teacher's chair by the stove. She watched Kirsten and her cousins as they walked to the benches on the girls' side of the room. But she didn't smile a welcome.

"We have a new teacher," Lisbeth whispered as she and Kirsten sat down.

The young teacher stood and tapped the stove with a ruler to get everyone's attention. Her dark hair was parted cleanly in the middle, her chin was up, her shoulders were back like a soldier's. "I am Miss Winston," she said in a crisp voice. "I've come west from Camden, Maine. I'm to be your teacher because Mr. Coogan was injured when his horse threw him." She looked around to see if all the students had heard her.

"I hope his horse stepped on him, too!" a black-haired boy said out loud.

"That's Amos Anderson!" Lisbeth whispered.

Miss Winston faced Amos. "You will not talk out of turn in my classroom. Although we live in the woods, we are not savages like the Indians."

"You will not talk out of turn in my classroom,"
Miss Winston said.

Amos grinned and looked down at his big hands. He had broad shoulders and the beginnings of a black mustache. Kirsten thought he looked more like a man than a boy.

"Now you know my name," Miss Winston continued. "But I don't know yours. I'd like each of you to come forward and introduce yourself to me politely. We are ladies and gentlemen here at Powderkeg School."

Anna was the first of the girls to go forward. She made a quick curtsy and said, "Anna Larson, ma'am."

Miss Winston nodded. "Very good. Next, please."

Kirsten tried to remember the names of the girls, but her head buzzed like a hive of bees. She didn't want to walk out there in the middle of the room with everyone watching her. She was the last girl to take her turn. The floor seemed to move under her as she stepped forward. She kept her gaze on her dusty boots as she made her curtsy.

"Kirsten Larson," she muttered.

Before she could escape back to the bench, Miss Winston said firmly, "Say 'Kirsten Larson, *ma'am.*'"

"Ma'am," Kirsten repeated. But the word didn't sound right. She felt a blush prickle at the base of her throat.

Miss Winston bent to look Kirsten right in the eye. "Do you speak English?" she asked.

"A little, ma'am." The buzz in Kirsten's ears was so loud she could hardly hear her own words. But she heard one of the girls giggle at her halting English.

"She's our cousin, Miss Winston!" Anna said. "She came to America last summer. We speak Swedish at home, ma'am."

Miss Winston raised her eyebrows and said, "Ah! Well, you will speak English in school, Kirsten. And you will begin with the easiest lessons. Anna will share her book with you and help you. Do you understand?"

Kirsten nodded.

"Say, 'I understand, ma'am,'" Miss Winston reminded her. "If you're going to learn English, you must practice. Practice makes perfect."

Now it was Amos who laughed at Kirsten.

Miss Winston's eyes narrowed, and she motioned for Kirsten to sit down again on the bench. Then Miss Winston whirled around, raised her ruler over her head, and brought it smashing down on the top of the iron stove. The crack went through the room like the shot of a rifle.

"My father could not be a ship's captain if he weren't in charge of his crew. I couldn't be a teacher if I weren't in charge of my students."

 Again she raised the ruler high and smacked the stove. "This is your first lesson," she said. " 'Miss Winston hit the stove.' *Miss Winston* is the subject of that sentence. *Hit* is the verb. The direct object of *hit* is *the stove*. Be careful that the direct object of *hit* isn't *the student*. Do you have any questions?"

No one said a single thing.

"Good. Now, you boys please come and introduce yourselves. Remember, you are gentlemen, not savages."

The littlest boys went first. They spoke their names and bowed. Even Peter, who was only five, took his turn easily. He'd learned a lot of English without even seeming to try, Kirsten thought.

It was Lars' turn. He said, "I'm Lars Larson,

10

ma'am," in a loud voice that everyone could hear easily. Lars wasn't afraid of anything, not even this teacher who seemed so strict. Mama had cut his hair last night, and it hugged his head like a bright cap.

Amos, with his dark mustache and eyes the color of blue paint, came last. He was much taller than Miss Winston. He looked as tall as Uncle Olav. "Amos Anderson, *ma'am*," he said. He bobbed his head instead of bowing.

"Which reading book are you using, Amos?" Miss Winston asked him.

"I finished the third one, *ma'am*." He winked at the girls' bench.

"Only the third? How old are you?" Miss Winston asked.

"I'm nineteen," Amos drawled. "Same as you." Miss Winston tapped her palm with her ruler and considered him. "Yes, Amos, I am nineteen, too. But I am the teacher and you are the student. I'm here to help you read and do sums the way a man must if he wants to make his way in the world. Please set a good example for the others."

Amos' face turned red. He looked at Miss

Winston closely. "Why don't I go draw a bucket of water so that the children can all have a drink before we start in reading," he said.

"Thank you, Amos. That's a good idea," Miss Winston said. Amos grabbed one of the wooden buckets. Through the small window, Kirsten saw him run like a deer toward the stream.

Miss Winston stood with her back to the door. "While we wait for our drink of water, we'll sing a song. Singing is very good exercise. It brings fresh air into our lungs." Keeping time with her ruler, she sang

"Be it ever so humble,
There's no place like home."

Her voice was firm and clear. Everyone sang along.

Home—the word was as sweet as clover honey on Kirsten's lips. How she wished she were home in Sweden where she was comfortable, where she could be herself. Or home with Mama, in their cozy cabin. Or anywhere but here with Miss Winston, in Powderkeg School.

Soon the singing stopped, and Amos was back with the bucket of water. He set it on the bench and handed Anna the dipper so she could get a drink. "Girls first," he said, as though he were in charge here, not Miss Winston. If Miss Winston minded, she didn't show it. She was busy passing out the books, small slates, and slate pencils.

Anna leaned against Kirsten's shoulder and opened her book to the alphabet section. She ran her finger down the page to the picture of a dog. " 'D. Dog.' Doesn't this dog look just like our Brownie when he smells a fox?" Anna said. "See, here are the letters that spell 'dog.' Copy them on your slate like I do."

Kirsten took her slate and did as Anna told her to. Once in a while Anna licked her finger, erased one of Kirsten's letters, and had her start again. Kirsten pressed her tongue against her upper lip and tried hard. Around her the other children worked at their reading. Some of them read out loud.

When Miss Winston came to check Kirsten's work, she said, "It seems Anna is a good teacher. Can you read what you've written here?"

"Dog," Kirsten said proudly. She hoped Miss Winston might say she'd done well.

13

Instead, Miss Winston pointed to Anna's slate. "You must learn to write 'The dog can run,' as Anna has done," she said.

"I love school, don't you?" Anna whispered.

Kirsten glanced up at the dusty windowpanes. It was still early morning. The first day of school was going to be a long one. She sighed and wrote again on her slate.

At last the first day of school was over. On their way home, Kirsten and her cousins stopped to play in their fort under the cherry tree. Anna fetched the dolls she'd hidden that morning.

Anna and Lisbeth's rag dolls had pretty painted faces. But Kirsten's doll didn't even have a face. It was an outgrown stocking stuffed with milkweed floss. Kirsten's real doll, Sari, was still in the painted trunk they had to store in Riverton. Kirsten missed her Sari so much that she named her sock doll Little Sari.

"Hello, children!" Anna said to the dolls in her high voice. "Come introduce yourselves like ladies!" To Kirsten she said, "Do you think Miss Winston is nice?"

"I don't know," Kirsten said. "She likes you, Anna. I don't think she likes me. And remember how she scolded?"

"Yes, she was fierce," Anna said.

"Is that what Mr. Coogan was like?" Kirsten asked.

"No, he was *much* worse," Lisbeth answered.

"Let's play school," Anna suggested. She patted down the long soft grass and picked out three red sumac leaves for benches. The girls sat their dolls down in a row.

"We'll pretend it's lunchtime," Kirsten said. She thought lunch had been the only good part of the school day. After she ate her bread and cheese and sausage, she played tree tag with the others in the school yard. In tag it didn't matter that Kirsten couldn't speak English well, because she was one of the fastest runners.

Now Lisbeth placed a little cake made of dried mud in front of each doll. "Here's your lunch,

children," she said. One mud cake was decorated
with gooseberries, one with acorn caps, one with
sunflower seeds in a star pattern.

Anna clapped her hands and scolded the dolls.
"No, no, children! Don't eat so fast! Remember you
are not savages like the Indians!" She sounded
exactly like Miss Winston.

When Kirsten laughed she lost some of the
flutters that had been in her stomach all day.
"What does 'savage' mean?" she asked Lisbeth.

Lisbeth made a scary face and pretended her
hands were scratching claws. "Savage means wild!"

16

"Are the Indians really savage?" Kirsten asked.

"Some people say the Indians are kind," Lisbeth said as she gave her doll a second cake. "They say the Indians gave them deer meat and corn when they needed food. But other people say the Indians are cruel and bloodthirsty."

"An Indian came to our door once, when Mama was roasting pork," Anna said. "Mama gave him a piece of meat and he went away."

"He didn't hurt us, but he didn't say 'thank you,' either," Lisbeth said.

"He *looked* savage," Anna said. "He had red paint on his cheeks and eagle feathers in his hair. He didn't wear trousers. And we didn't hear him coming. We looked up and suddenly he was in the doorway." Anna's eyes were wide. "That's Indian magic."

Lisbeth laughed. "That's not magic, Anna. They wear soft shoes, that's all."

"They wear long knives, too," Anna said. She shivered and hugged her doll. "And they live in tents."

"Papa worries about the Indians," Lisbeth said. "He says that if we plant crops on their hunting land the wild animals will go away. He says the Indians won't have enough to eat then, and they'll surely be angry. I don't know . . ." Her voice trailed off and she looked at Kirsten with her gray eyes. "Papa says we need the land, too."

"Do the Indians live in their tents all winter? Don't they get cold?" asked Kirsten.

"I don't know," Lisbeth said. "You're too curious, Kirsten! Let's just play school."

A SECRET FRIEND

A few days later Miss Winston opened class by saying, "I have good news for you today." Her face was flushed and she held her hands behind her back as though she hid a present there. "We are going to do something special in Powderkeg School this year! Each one of you will learn a poem. When you've memorized it, you will stand here by the stove and recite it to your classmates. If you do an excellent job, you'll earn a Reward of Merit."

Kirsten slipped down in her seat. Oh, this was too much. Even if she learned to read a poem, how could she remember it? And if she did manage somehow to remember it, how could she stand there in Miss Winston's place and say the words out loud?

"Just saying your poem is not enough, of course," Miss Winston went on. There was excitement in her voice. "You must speak with feeling! If your poem expresses anger, you must do *this.*" She stretched out her neck and turned down her lips.

A few of the boys tried that, and laughed until she frowned at them.

"If your poem expresses love, you must do *this.*" Now Miss Winston smoothed her forehead, smiled gently, and lowered her eyelids. "There are many feelings to express. This is excellent training for your young minds, believe me."

Kirsten chewed on her knuckle. Flutters had come back into her stomach again.

Miss Winston walked among the students, giving everyone a different poem. When she got to Kirsten, she paged to the back of the first reading book. "Oh, here's a good one for you, Kirsten. It's not too long, and it will give you a chance to show both anger and love. You're a lucky girl!" She pointed to the poem.

To Kirsten the words seemed to swim on the page like tadpoles in the stream. When Miss Winston moved on, Kirsten said, "Quick, Anna, read it to me."

Anna read:

>"Coo, coo, says the gentle dove,
>Coo, coo, says its little mate;
>They play with each other in love,
>And never show anger or hate."

As Anna read, Kirsten tried very hard not to cry. But tears came to her eyes. How could she ever learn all these words? She wished she could just vanish from Powderkeg School like a ghost disappearing into the night.

The next morning, when Kirsten went down to the stream to fetch Mama a bucket of water, a V of geese was flying south. She stopped on the path to watch the geese. Then she stopped again when she came upon a deer drinking at the stream.

She stood very still and waited for the deer to finish drinking. Then she heard a bird's whistle. She looked across the stream. Turtles sunned on a fallen log. A frog jumped into the water. Then, among the cattails, she saw a dark face watching her—dark eyes, black hair, the fringed sleeve of a deerskin dress. An Indian girl stood right there!

Kirsten held her breath. The Indian girl looked at her without blinking.

"Hello," Kirsten said softly.

The Indian girl didn't speak or move. But the word startled the deer away into the pines. When Kirsten looked back from the deer for the Indian girl, she was gone.

Kirsten thought maybe she'd only imagined the girl had been there. Maybe her eyes had played tricks on her. She crossed the stream on the stones and walked a little way into the cattails. No one. But when she went back to the shore, she saw there was a footprint in the soft sand. The footprint was a little smaller than the print left by her own boots. And near the footprint was a blue bead no larger than a gooseberry. The girl must have dropped it.

Kirsten stooped and picked up the bead. She wrapped it in her hankie and put it deep into her apron pocket. As she filled her bucket with water, Kirsten wondered if the girl had been sent here for water, too. Kirsten wanted to meet her. How could she do that? Would the girl come again?

Kirsten had an idea. She set down her bucket, hurried into the woods, and crawled into the fort.
 She took one of the doll cakes decorated with a circle of tiny snail shells. Then she crossed the stream again and laid the doll cake on the sand by the girl's footprints. If the Indian girl came back to the stream, maybe she'd find the doll cake. If she did, she'd know it was Kirsten who left it there.

When Kirsten got back to the cabin, her breakfast waited for her on the table. Mama scolded, "You were gone so long I thought you'd lost your way. Lars and Peter have already left for school. Hurry, or you'll be late."

All day Kirsten wondered about the Indian girl. When Kirsten went back to the stream after supper, the doll cake was gone. In its place was the green

wing feather of a duck, stuck into the sand like a little flag. Kirsten smiled as she picked up the duck feather and put it into her hankie with the bead. Maybe there was a way to make friends with the dark-eyed girl.

Every morning and every evening when she went for water, Kirsten looked for the Indian girl. Kirsten practiced walking very quietly through the woods in the hope that she might surprise her. Maybe the girl hid in the cattails, watching her. Kirsten didn't know exactly when the girl came to the stream, but she knew when she'd been there. Because every time Kirsten left a gift on the shore, the girl took it and left something in its place.

Once Kirsten left a piece of red yarn wrapped around a white pebble. In its place she found a length of leather thong as smooth as silk.

Kirsten left a little doll she'd shaped from mud, with a leaf stuck on for a skirt. That night she found a tiny basket woven of grass where the doll had been.

Kirsten left a green button on a loop of green thread. It was replaced by a purple bead.

Kirsten strung the two beads on the leather thong. She kept them wrapped in her hankie with the feather and the tiny basket. These were her secret treasures, and the Indian girl was her secret friend. At school, when Kirsten was tired of writing and numbers, of trying to learn her poem and trying to please Miss Winston, she daydreamed of running off across the prairie with the Indian girl. They wouldn't need to talk. They'd run faster than the wind.

How Kirsten wanted to see the mysterious girl again! One evening she saved her slice of bread and honey from supper. She wrapped the honey sandwich in oak leaves. Then she went to the stream for water. She put the package of oak leaves on the other shore, then settled down to wait. Maybe the Indian girl came here at dusk. Kirsten decided she would meet her, no matter what.

But the sun was almost down. Kirsten wasn't allowed to stay away from the cabin after sunset—Mama would worry. "Please come," Kirsten whispered under her breath, as though that would make the Indian girl appear.

And then, there she was! In her dress of soft deerskin, the Indian girl slipped silently through the cattails. She stooped and picked up the oak leaf package. She peeled off the leaves, sniffed, and began to eat the bread and honey. As she ate she looked right at Kirsten. Kirsten didn't speak. She didn't want to frighten the girl away again. Instead, she walked slowly forward, watching the girl.

The girl was a little smaller than Kirsten. Her hair and skin shone as if they'd been polished. Kirsten thought she'd never seen eyes so inky black. The Indian girl licked honey from her finger. She watched Kirsten, too.

Dark shadows moved on the stream as Kirsten crossed the stones. When she stood in front of the Indian girl, the girl reached into the leather pouch she wore around her waist. She held out to Kirsten a tiny clay pot decorated with markings that might have been made from a sharp twig.

Kirsten took the little pot. It was as small as an acorn. "It's pretty!" she breathed.

The Indian girl looked at her hard. Slowly, as though she feared she would scare Kirsten, she reached out and touched Kirsten's yellow braid.

*Slowly, the Indian girl
reached out and touched Kirsten's yellow braid.*

Then she touched the other one.

Kirsten was so pleased that she laughed. She held out the little pot again and repeated, "Pretty!"

The Indian girl couldn't seem to take her gaze from Kirsten's yellow hair. Again, she stroked one of Kirsten's looped braids.

Kirsten touched the girl's beaded necklace. Oh, if only they could talk to each other! "Pretty," Kirsten said. "Pretty."

The girl's eyes were as unblinking as a deer's. She touched Kirsten's apron, which was decorated with a cross-stitched border. She said something— what was it? "Tee. Pur. Tee."

She's saying "pretty," Kirsten thought. She wished she could take off her apron and give it to the girl. But Mama would be angry if Kirsten came home without her apron. So instead, she took her hankie from her pocket, opened the little bundle, and showed the girl the gifts she'd saved. The girl made a pleased purring sound deep in her throat.

Kirsten put the gifts and the little pot into her apron pocket. She held out her hankie to the girl. The hankie had a cross-stitched border in blue and red—Kirsten had sewed it herself.

"Here, *pretty*," she said.

The Indian girl took the hankie. "Pur-tee," she repeated after Kirsten.

Then Kirsten realized that it was almost night. If she didn't hurry, she wouldn't get back to the cabin before dark. Quickly, Kirsten bent down and drew in the sand. She made a setting sun. Then she pointed to where the red sun was sinking down beyond the trees.

The girl looked at the sun, then at the drawing. She squatted and drew a picture just like Kirsten's in the sand. Now there were two suns side by side.

Kirsten touched each one. "Will you come tomorrow when the sun is like this?" she asked.

The Indian girl only stared at her. She touched the hankie Kirsten had given her to her cheek. Then she turned and was swiftly gone into the cattails along the stream.

VISITORS

"Miss Winston's coming to live at our house!" Lisbeth said proudly.

Kirsten was walking to school with Lisbeth and Anna. "Oh, no!" she replied.

"It's an *honor*, Kirsten," Lisbeth said. "We've never had a teacher live with us."

"But we didn't *want* Mr. Coogan," Anna added. She wrapped her shawl more tightly, because the November days were turning colder.

Kirsten's spirits sank. The best part of the school day was when she left Powderkeg School and headed home. If Miss Winston came to Lisbeth's and Anna's, it would be as though school followed her home.

But Anna was so excited she skipped. "Won't it be grand! Miss Winston will eat supper with us every night. She'll have a bed up in the loft near ours. Papa hung up a curtain to make her a little room."

Lisbeth laced her arm through Kirsten's. "Miss Winston's been living in a shed off the Engberg's kitchen, but now the shed is too cold. She says our house will be wonderful. She's heard our mama is a good cook."

"Well, there's no room for her in our cabin," Kirsten said firmly. "Anyway, my mama doesn't speak any English at all." In the chill air her breath made little clouds at her lips.

"But that's the best part!" Anna went on. "You and your family will eat with us more often. Your mama will cook with mine, and we'll all have supper together. That way your mama and papa can learn more English. Papa says that with Miss Winston at the table, it won't be polite to speak Swedish."

Now Kirsten's spirits sank even lower. The happiest time for her family was when they sat down together for supper. Papa talked about the crops and the animals. Mama spoke of the wool she was spinning. She almost had enough to begin weaving. Lars and Peter joked about the pranks the boys played at recess. How could they speak of these things if they struggled with English?

And Kirsten didn't want to have school lessons at suppertime, too. Would Miss Winston smack her ruler on Uncle Olav's table as she did on the stove at school?

"When is she coming?" Kirsten asked.

"Next Sunday," Lisbeth said.

Quickly, Kirsten counted the days. This was Tuesday, so there were only five more nights of freedom left.

"Just think," Anna said, "she'll dress right in our room! I bet she has beautiful petticoats. She's a lady, you know. Ladies wear beautiful underclothes, I'm sure of it."

Kirsten scowled. "Anna, I don't care what kind of underclothes Miss Winston wears!" But when she saw Anna's lower lip tremble, she took her cousin's arm. "I didn't mean to hurt your feelings."

"You're probably cross because you've had

such a hard time remembering your poem," Lisbeth said.

That comment didn't make Kirsten feel any better. She put her hand into her apron pocket, where she kept the gifts Singing Bird had given her. That was the Indian girl's name: Singing Bird. She and Kirsten were already the best of friends. Every day, they'd explore the woods and the caves along the stream. Singing Bird taught Kirsten to whistle like a meadowlark. When Kirsten was with Singing Bird, she felt as free as the rabbits they scattered as they ran. She felt as strong and swift as the young deer they often came upon in the woods. She forgot to worry about trying to fit in at school, about trying to learn her lessons, about trying to speak English correctly.

That afternoon there were long shadows under the pines when Kirsten ran to the stream with the bucket bumping her leg. Singing Bird waited for her under a willow tree.

"Hello!" Kirsten said.

Singing Bird touched Kirsten's blonde braid, as she liked to do. "Ho," she said.

Kirsten beckoned for Singing Bird to follow her farther into the woods. For several days, Kirsten had planned to take Singing Bird to the doll fort under the cherry tree. Lisbeth and Anna might be cross if Kirsten took someone into the fort without their permission—especially an Indian. But Kirsten had decided to take a chance.

Singing Bird crawled behind Kirsten through the tunnel into the fort. Red leaves carpeted the ground there. A raccoon peered at the girls from the lowest branch of the cherry tree. The yellowed grass inside the fort was still thick, and all the doll furniture was there.

Singing Bird's eyes grew wide when Kirsten showed her the stacks of doll cakes and cookies. "Purtee!" she said. She touched the three doll beds of woven twigs, the doll blankets woven from scraps of cotton, and the little cross Lisbeth had made so they could pretend their dolls went to church. Kirsten took the tiny basket and clay pot from her pocket. She put them on the table with the doll cakes. She pretended to drink from the pot, then offered it to Singing Bird.

Singing Bird gathered a few bare twigs and tied

them together at one end with a strand of grass. She set the twigs upright on the moss and wrapped a large oak leaf around them. "Tepee," she told Kirsten. Then she walked her fingers into the tepee. "Come," she said.

Kirsten laughed with pleasure. She put the small basket and pot into the tepee. Then she walked her fingers inside, as Singing Bird had done. "Here I am," she said.

Singing Bird shook her head. "*My* tepee." She stood and stretched her arms wide to show Kirsten she spoke of a real tepee.

Kirsten's heart sped up. Singing Bird wanted her to go to the Indian village! Kirsten knew the Indian village was close by, but she didn't know where. Lars said he had seen the tepees when he was out setting traps for rabbits. But none of the children at school had been there. Most of them did not trust Indians. Of course, they didn't know Singing Bird.

"Where is your tepee?" Kirsten asked.

Singing Bird pointed toward the ridge where the sun was setting.

"My tepee."
Singing Bird stretched her arms wide.

"Yes! I'll come!" Kirsten said.

But she knew that it was too late to go today. Every day the sun set earlier, and the sky was already getting dark now. So she added, "I'll come *soon.*" Then she put the doll furniture back in place, and Singing Bird untied the small tepee and scattered the twigs. They walked back to the stream together.

Instead of drawing a setting sun as a promise to meet tomorrow, Singing Bird drew a full sun and pointed to the east. She meant for them to meet in the morning. Kirsten shook her head, then drew two suns like Singing Bird's. She meant she couldn't come tomorrow, but she would be there the next day, before she went to school. She would meet Singing Bird and go to her village. Kirsten didn't know how she'd get away, but she knew she would.

Then, as she could do so easily, Singing Bird vanished into the shadowy grove and was gone.

SINGING BIRD
AND YELLOW HAIR

Miss Winston stopped next to Kirsten's seat and tapped the back of the log bench with her ruler. "I don't believe you're really *trying*," the teacher scolded. "Why can't you learn your poem?"

Kirsten bit her lip. "I *am* trying, ma'am," she said.

"Please look at me when I speak to you," Miss Winston said.

Kirsten forced herself to look up. She thought that if Miss Winston didn't look so stern she would be very pretty.

"Can you *read* the words of your poem?" Miss Winston asked. She pointed to the lines which

Kirsten had been trying all week to memorize.

"I can read the words, but I can't remember them," Kirsten murmured.

"Your cousin Lisbeth recited all thirty-two lines of 'To a Waterfowl.' I'm only asking you to memorize these few lines. Your memory is like a muscle, Kirsten. You must use it to make it strong."

Kirsten nodded unhappily. Her poor mind felt like a tired muscle. When she tried to say her poem without looking at the book, the words seemed to disappear like geese flying into the mist.

It seemed everyone could memorize and recite except Kirsten. Amos Anderson had learned a whole poem. He recited it with his voice galloping along like the horses and the battle he described. Miss Winston had smiled proudly when she handed him a Reward of Merit. Kirsten thought that Miss Winston was proud of everyone but her.

"You *must* try harder," Miss Winston said firmly. "If at first you don't succeed, try, try again."

Kirsten thought that even if she could memorize her poem, she was sure to forget it when she stood up in front of the class. If she forgot, she might cry. That would be the worst thing of all.

The next morning, Kirsten got up extra early and rushed through her chores. "Why are you in such a hurry?" Mama asked. She put out several thin pancakes and a slice of ham for Kirsten's breakfast.

Kirsten wrapped the ham in a pancake. "I'll eat on the way to school. I'm going early to practice saying my verse."

"You've learned a verse in English? Oh, you're a smart girl, Kirsten," Mama said with a big smile.

"Go on, then, if you're doing schoolwork," Papa said.

Kirsten ran for the door. "Tell Lisbeth and Anna I'm practicing. I'll meet them at school," she said. She knew it was wrong to lie to Mama and Papa, but she couldn't help herself. As she ran to meet Singing Bird she *tried* to say her poem so the lie wouldn't be such a bad one.

As soon as she heard Singing Bird whistle, Kirsten forgot all about the poem and her lie. She

40

handed Singing Bird the pancake and the meat, and the girl ate gladly. Then Singing Bird said, "Come."

Kirsten ran behind Singing Bird through the long, pale prairie grass. Crows flew up beside them, and rabbits scattered. Kirsten didn't even care how far they had to run. She was glad to be free from school, glad to be on this adventure with Singing Bird.

They ran through a grove of pines, then up a trail to the top of a hill. Down below, five big Indian tepees circled a large campfire. Nearby, spotted ponies grazed.

As the girls started down the hill to the village, scrawny Indian dogs ran barking to meet them. Then Indian children came from the tents. They spoke to Singing Bird in their language.

The children crowded around and wanted to touch Kirsten's blonde hair. One little boy crouched to touch her leather boots and their laces. Indian women came forward to look at Kirsten's apron, too. Their dark hands were gentle.

Singing Bird stood close by Kirsten's side. Then she said, "Come. Come to my father," and pointed to the tallest tepee.

Kirsten followed Singing Bird to the tepee. It was made of buffalo skins. Singing Bird lifted the flap that was its door. Inside, the tepee was dim and warm. When Kirsten's eyes adjusted to the gloom, she saw a man sitting cross-legged on a bear skin. Eagle feathers were braided into his hair, and he wore a necklace of bear claws.

"I am Brave Elk," he said in a deep voice.

"How do you do," Kirsten said, and remembered to curtsy.

"You are Singing Bird's friend," he said.

"Yes," Kirsten said. She touched Singing Bird's

arm to make sure she was at her side. "Singing Bird is my friend, too."

"You teach your English words to Singing Bird," Brave Elk said.

"My English words?" That surprised Kirsten. But she thought Brave Elk was right—she hadn't once thought of trying to speak Swedish with Singing Bird. "Singing Bird teaches me, too," Kirsten went on. "Tepee. Moccasin." She pointed to those things to show Brave Elk she knew what she said in his language.

The chief nodded. "Good. You are Yellow Hair. You are welcome here. You stay," he said.

He motioned to the woman who stood in the shadows. The woman gave Kirsten a piece of flat bread made from cornmeal.

Now Singing Bird led Kirsten to sit beside her on a pile of animal skins. She showed Kirsten her leather pouch which held a knife, a bone needle, and a length of sinew for sewing. She showed Kirsten her doll, which was made of soft buckskin and stuffed with grass.

Oh, how Kirsten wished she could live here in

43

this warm tent with Singing Bird. She would wear
soft moccasins like Singing Bird's. She would wear
a deerskin dress and leggings. She would sleep
under warm buffalo hides and play with a little
buckskin doll of her own. All day she and Singing
Bird would play in the fields and woods. Instead of
Kirsten Larson, who couldn't memorize her poem,
she would be Yellow Hair, Singing Bird's sister.

A little boy came into the tepee to show Kirsten
his wooden top. When he lifted the tent flap,
Kirsten saw that the sun had risen high in the sky.
She would have to run fast in order to get to school

on time. She touched Singing Bird's arm and
pointed to the sun. The girl said something to her
father, then held open the tent flap. "Come," she
said to Kirsten. And they ran back up the trail.

CHAPTER FIVE

BELONGING

It was Sunday night, and Miss Winston sat next to Uncle Olav at the table. It was her first meal with the Larsons.

Aunt Inger and Mama had made a big dinner to welcome her. They'd even baked ginger cookies, just like at Christmas.

"My parents have a lovely home on a harbor in Maine," Miss Winston said. "There's a small room on the top. It has windows on all four sides. When my father is at sea, we watch for his ship from that room."

"What a fine room that must be!" Anna said. She was the only one talking to Miss Winston.

Uncle Olav offered everyone more rabbit stew.

Mama kept busy cutting and passing bread.

"Why did you want to leave such a lovely home?" Anna asked. She was so excited to have Miss Winston there that she'd forgotten all about her supper.

 "Well, I certainly wasn't ready to marry and spend the rest of my life in a house," Miss Winston said. "I wanted to travel, to meet people, to have adventures! School teachers travel, so I decided to become a teacher. Maybe you will be a teacher when you grow up, Anna. You've been a good little teacher for Kirsten."

Kirsten kept her eyes on her tin plate. With Miss Winston at the table, it seemed she'd forgotten all the English she'd ever learned. And what if Mama or Papa said something to Miss Winston about the poem Kirsten said she had memorized? Miss Winston would say Kirsten hadn't done it. Kirsten's head ached at the thought.

Anna said, "Does your father sail on his ship every day?"

Miss Winston smiled. "No, Anna, he isn't a fisherman. He has a big ship for carrying heavy

47

cargo. He sails down the coast with a load of wool. Then he sails back with a load of tobacco."

"I might want to be a sailor," Lars said. "Life is exciting on a ship!"

Miss Winston looked at Lars. "Would you like to see my father's ship?"

"*Ja!*" Lars said. Then he reddened and corrected himself. "Yes, ma'am."

"Then after our meal, I'll show you a surprise," Miss Winston said.

"Eat, Anna," Uncle Olav commanded. "You'll get thin if you don't pay attention to your dinner."

After everyone had finished eating, Miss Winston left the table. She climbed the ladder to the loft where she'd put her things. In a moment she was back with a bottle in her hand. She set the bottle on its side in the middle of the table.

Everyone leaned forward to look. Inside the bottle was a model of a two-masted schooner. "This ship looks just like my father's," said Miss Winston.

Kirsten drew in a sharp breath. "It looks just like the *Eagle,* too!" she said.

Miss Winston handed Kirsten the bottle so she could get a better look. Now she saw the ship

48

Kirsten drew a sharp breath.
"It looks just like the Eagle, too!"

closely. "The ship we sailed on to America looked just like this one. It was called the *Eagle.* We sailed for ten weeks. There were terrible storms. Everyone was sick. Six people died on the ship, and the sailors buried them at sea." She stopped, breathless, surprised at how many words she had just blurted out in English.

Miss Winston pressed her forefinger to her lips and looked closely at Kirsten. "You remember the ship clearly, don't you?"

"Oh, yes! My friend Marta and I played on the deck," Kirsten said.

"Ah!" Miss Winston exclaimed. "You've given me an idea, Kirsten."

In school the next day, Miss Winston came to Kirsten's side right after the first song. She handed Kirsten a piece of paper. Kirsten sat up straight, her heart thudding. Miss Winston never gave out paper.

"Here is another poem for you, Kirsten. I want you to memorize it instead of the first one I gave you," Miss Winston said. "It's four lines from a long poem about a man who was a sailor all his life. When you spoke of your trip on the *Eagle,* I thought

you might like these lines. Can you read them?"

Miss Winston's writing was as perfect as the writing in a book. Kirsten held the paper in both hands and read slowly but clearly

"Swiftly, swiftly flew the ship
Yet she sailed softly too:
Sweetly, sweetly blew the breeze—
On me alone it blew."

As she read, Kirsten could almost feel the ocean wind on her face and taste the salt spray on her lips. And she missed Marta.

"You read that well, Kirsten. Do you think you

could memorize these lines?" Miss Winston asked.

Kirsten nodded. She hoped that if she forgot any words, she could imagine the *Eagle* and the words would come back to her. "I'll try," she said.

Miss Winston bent down until her eyes were level with Kirsten's. "You will try and you will succeed. Remember that, please." Then she went to open the door of the iron stove so Amos could put in more wood to heat the classroom.

Because Kirsten and her family ate dinner at Uncle Olav's house now, it was impossible for Kirsten to meet Singing Bird at their usual time in the evening. And there was never enough time in the morning. But on Wednesday Kirsten managed to leave a tiny doll made of yarn for her friend. After school, she found a piece of blue and white beadwork in its place. She thought it would make a beautiful headband for Sari.

Beside the beads, Singing Bird had drawn a full sun in the sand. She wanted Kirsten to come early in the morning to meet her. Sadly, Kirsten drew a cross through the drawing to tell Singing Bird that she couldn't come. When would she be able to meet her friend again?

On Friday, Kirsten whispered to Miss Winston that she was ready to recite her verse. Her chest ached and her stomach fluttered, but she wanted to recite before she forgot the poem.

Miss Winston held up her hand and told everyone to be still. "Kirsten Larson will now recite. Please come forward, Kirsten." Miss Winston stepped back so that Kirsten could stand in front of the stove where everyone would see her.

Slowly, Kirsten walked to the center of the room. She tried to keep her chin high, just like Miss Winston did. She saw Anna's smile and Lars' grin. Then the room seemed to blur and fade, and all she heard was the thud of her heart.

"You may recite now," Miss Winston said. "With feeling, please."

Now, Kirsten told herself. She imagined the sails of the *Eagle* creaking overhead. She imagined sea gulls swooping and diving in the wind. She imagined Marta sitting by her side on the deck.

*She kept her eyes closed and
recited the poem without a single mistake.*

"Swiftly, swiftly flew the ship," Kirsten said. She heard her own words clearly, as though someone else had spoken them. She kept her eyes closed and recited the poem without a single mistake.

When she opened her eyes the other students were smiling at her. Miss Winston touched her shoulder. "You recited very well, Kirsten. You recited with feeling. I'm proud of you," she said.

Kirsten sat down in a daze. She had stood in front of everyone and recited her poem in English! She hadn't thought she could do it, but she had. And it hadn't been so hard, after all. The next time would be easier, she was sure of it. She'd been scared, but she had done it, and now Miss Winston was proud of her.

Anna nudged her and said, "Good for you!" Lisbeth gave her a wink that said the same thing.

"Now it's time for reading," Miss Winston said.

But Kirsten was too dizzy to read. "May I fetch the water for our drink?" she asked Miss Winston.

"Yes, Kirsten, thank you. As you walk, don't forget to take deep breaths to draw fresh air into your lungs," Miss Winston said with a smile.

Kirsten seized the bucket and her shawl.

Outside, the air was cold. A light dusting of snow lay on the ground. When she reached the stream, Kirsten found a thin coat of ice on the water.

She broke the ice easily with a stick and dipped her bucket into the stream. As she did, she heard the whistle of a meadowlark. When Kirsten looked up she saw Singing Bird standing among the ice-coated cattails on the other side of the stream.

"Hello!" Kirsten said.

"Come," Singing Bird answered.

"But I can't come with you now," Kirsten said. "I have to go back to school."

"Come," Singing Bird repeated. She crossed the stream on a fallen log.

"Maybe I can come after school," Kirsten said, though she wasn't sure how she could.

"Come *now*," Singing Bird replied. "We go today."

Kirsten grasped her friend's cold hand. "Go? You're going? But why?"

"No food," Singing Bird said. She pressed her hands to her stomach.

"Don't you have enough food?" Kirsten asked.
She remembered the terrible pains in her stomach
when Papa's crops had failed in Sweden. She
remembered how Peter had cried when there was
no more bread to eat.

"Bad hunting," Singing Bird explained. She
held up her arms as though she shot an arrow from
a bow. "We go to find food."

Kirsten remembered what Lisbeth and Anna
had told her. The wild animals were leaving the
land because the settlers were building farms. The
Indians didn't have enough to eat. They were
leaving to find more food.

"Where will you go?" Kirsten asked. When
Papa couldn't grow enough food in Sweden, they
had come here to America. Where could the Indians
go to find better hunting?

Singing Bird pointed west. "We go there. For
buffalo. For deer." Then she stroked the blonde

braids which looped Kirsten's ears.
"You come too," Singing Bird said.

Kirsten looked at the snow-covered
hill where a hawk circled in the sky.
Then she looked at her friend's dark

face, so close to her own.

"Come, sister," Singing Bird said. She took Kirsten's hand.

Kirsten remembered the warm tepee where Singing Bird lived. She imagined herself sleeping by Singing Bird's side under the buffalo hides. If she lived with Singing Bird she would be free to roam the woods all day. Brave Elk would be good to her. He was the chief, and Kirsten would be his yellow-haired daughter. She and Singing Bird would always be together.

But how could Kirsten leave her own parents, her brothers, her cousins? How could she leave the cabin under the pines? If she didn't come back home, Mama and Papa would be wild with worry. They would think she was lost. They might even think she'd been killed. And they would never give her permission to go with Singing Bird.

"No. I *can't* come with you," Kirsten said. "I want to come, but this is my home. I can't leave my home," Kirsten said.

Singing Bird looked down sadly. She reached into the pouch she wore around her waist and took

out her bone needle. She gave it to Kirsten.

Kirsten closed her hand around the bone needle. "Will you come back, Singing Bird?"

Singing Bird shook her head. "If deer come back," she said.

"Oh, please, do come back!" Kirsten said. "I'll be here. Right here. You can find me easily. Whistle for me by the stream."

"If deer come back," Singing Bird repeated. She touched Kirsten's braid one last time. Then she ran back to the fallen log and crossed the stream. She waved from the edge of the pine forest before she disappeared into the snow-covered trees.

Kirsten watched her friend go. She imagined Singing Bird's tribe hungry, wandering, looking for

food. Where would they go? How far would they have to travel before they could set up their village again? Now Kirsten understood that if the settlers made a home here, the Indians would have to find a new home.

She filled her water bucket and trudged slowly back to the school. She pushed open the door to the warm room. Miss Winston looked up from her place by the stove. "You've been gone a long time, Kirsten. I thought you'd found that ship in your poem and sailed back to Sweden!"

"No, ma'am," Kirsten said softly. She knew it was a joke, but she was too sad to smile. She slipped her hand into her pocket and touched the bone needle. How she would miss Singing Bird!

Miss Winston smiled, though. "I left something for you. It's in your reader," she said.

Kirsten looked around the cozy room crowded with busy children. She wasn't sure when this place had become her own, but she belonged here now.

Her reader lay on the bench waiting for her.

"Will you help me again?" she asked Anna.

"Yes!" Anna said gladly, as she always did, and made room on the bench. Kirsten sat down and opened her book.

LOOKING BACK 1854

A PEEK INTO
THE PAST

Farm family, 1888

Pioneer children like Kirsten didn't start school every year in September like you do. Instead, during the fall they were busy working on the farm. They picked apples, husked corn, carried water, and cooked for the hungry men who were working in the fields. They helped preserve fruits and vegetables, and they gathered firewood to smoke the meat that had been butchered. They worked very hard until November when the harvest was over. Then, when the farm was ready for winter, it was time for them to go back to school.

Pioneer schools like Kirsten's

were open only in the winter
and summer. Children had to
help at home with the harvest
in the fall and the plowing
and planting in the spring.
Some children—especially
older boys who worked in the

Frontier school, 1854

fields—didn't go to school during the summer, either.
And they often skipped school in the winter, too,
if there was farm work to do.

In a school like Kirsten's, students of all ages were
in the same room with the same teacher. The youngest
students were three or four years old. The oldest were
sometimes older than the teacher. Students in one-
room schools were not divided into grades by age.

Country school students, 1895

Instead, they all worked on the same subject at the same time, but they used different books.

A new teacher like Miss Winston could tell how well students read just by finding out which book they were using. The first reader—the one that Kirsten and Anna shared—taught the letters of the alphabet and used pictures to help students learn simple words. After the alphabet lessons came very short stories. Students learned to read with expression by using books like this. When the words went up, students were supposed to

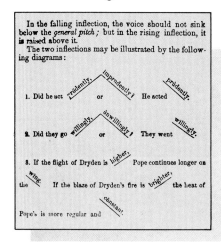

make their voices go higher. When the words went down, voices were supposed to go lower.

A student reciting

Students in pioneer schools also learned to write and do *sums*, or arithmetic. They memorized rules of grammar and important dates in American history, and they practiced *recitation*, or speaking before the class.

The teacher in a one-room school worked with one or two pupils at a time. While she was busy with those students, she expected the others to work alone or to help one another. Books were hard to get on the frontier, so students shared them. Paper was scarce, so students usually recited their lessons out loud instead of writing them down. Because everyone talked at once, pioneer schools were sometimes called *blab schools.*

When students needed to write, they used slates which could be erased and used again. They shared their slates, just as they shared their books. If there weren't enough slates to go around, younger students might learn to write by tracing letters in the ground outside the schoolhouse door—or on the classroom floor itself, if it was made of dirt instead

of wood. Most frontier schools did not have equipment like maps, charts, globes, or even blackboards.

Students like Kirsten did not work at desks. They sat on wooden benches that circled the pot-

bellied stove in the middle of the room. When they were called on to recite, they stood in front of the teacher. It was easy for everyone in the room to know that a student had recited poorly, because the teacher would hit her desk—or the student—with a ruler, a leather strap, or a willow switch. When a student did well, the teacher would give out a *Reward of Merit*. Since paper and printed things were scarce on the frontier, the pretty certificate was a reward indeed.

There were not many rewards for pioneer teachers, though. Besides preparing lessons, a teacher had to keep the one-room school neat and start the fire in the stove every morning. In some schools, the teacher had to chop and stack firewood, too. Teachers on the frontier did not earn much money. They were usually paid between four and ten dollars a month. Most teachers did not have homes of their own. Instead, they *boarded round*—they lived with the families of their students, moving from house to house during the school year.

A pioneer schoolteacher

Teachers may have been discouraged sometimes. It was hard to teach in an organized way when many students came to school only once in a while, if they weren't too busy with farm chores. And it was a challenge to teach students like Kirsten, who couldn't speak or write much English. But like Miss Winston, pioneer teachers knew that their job was an important one and they were determined to do it well.